STONE ARCH BOOKS
a capstone imprint

THE BATMAN STRIKES!

STONE ARCH BOOKS™

Published in 2015 by Stone Arch Books
A Capstone Imprint
1710 Roe Crest Drive
North Mankato, MN 56003
www.capstonepub.com

Originally published by DC Comics in the U.S. in
single magazine form as The Batman Strikes! #12.

DC Comics
1700 Broadway, New York, NY 10019
A Warner Bros. Entertainment Company

Printed in China by Nordica.
0914/CA21401510
092014 008470NORDS15

Cataloging-in-Publication Data is available at the
Library of Congress website.
ISBN: 978-1-4342-9665-8 (library binding)

Summary: Bane is out for revenge, trying to find
the doctor who turned him into a monster. When
Batman tries to intervene, will Bane overcome
him? Or will Batman finally defeat Bane?

STONE ARCH BOOKS

Ashley C. Andersen Zantop *Publisher*
Michael Dahl *Editorial Director*
Eliza Leahy *Editor*
Heather Kindseth *Creative Director*
Peggie Carley *Designer*
Tori Abraham *Production Specialist*

DC COMICS

Nachie Castro *Original U.S. Editor*

BANE'S BREAKING IN!

BILL MATHENY ....WRITER

CHRISTOPHER JONES ....PENCILLER

TERRY BEATTY ....INKER

HEROIC AGE...COLORIST

PHIL BALSMAN..LETTERER

BATMAN CREATED BY BOB KANE

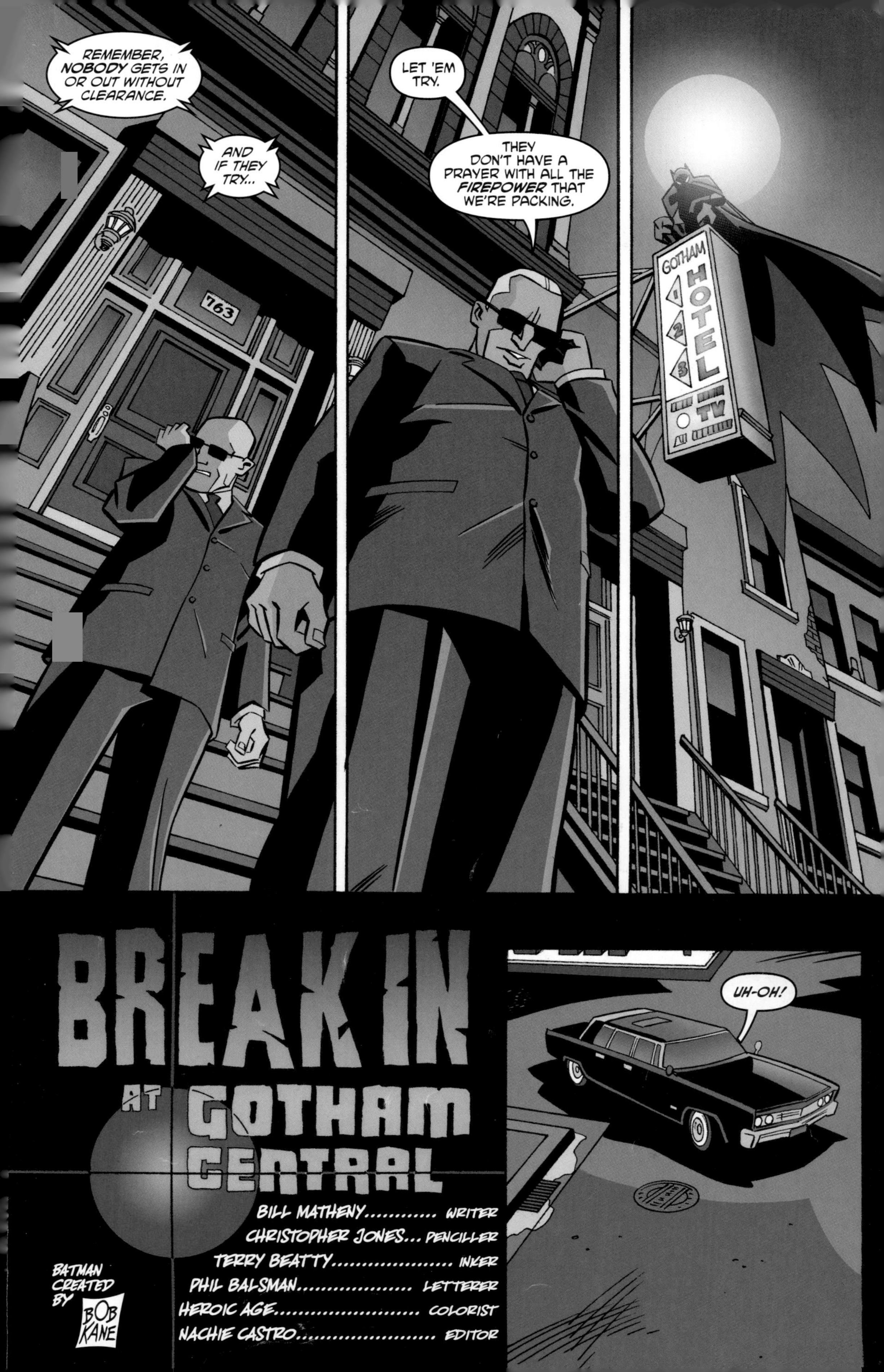
REMEMBER, NOBODY GETS IN OR OUT WITHOUT CLEARANCE.
AND IF THEY TRY...
763
LET 'EM TRY.
THEY DON'T HAVE A PRAYER WITH ALL THE FIREPOWER THAT WE'RE PACKING.
GOTHAM
HOTEL
TV
BREAK IN AT GOTHAM CENTRAL
BILL MATHENY............ WRITER
CHRISTOPHER JONES... PENCILLER
TERRY BEATTY..................... INKER
PHIL BALSMAN.................. LETTERER
HEROIC AGE......................... COLORIST
NACHIE CASTRO........................ EDITOR
BATMAN CREATED BY BOB KANE
UH-OH!

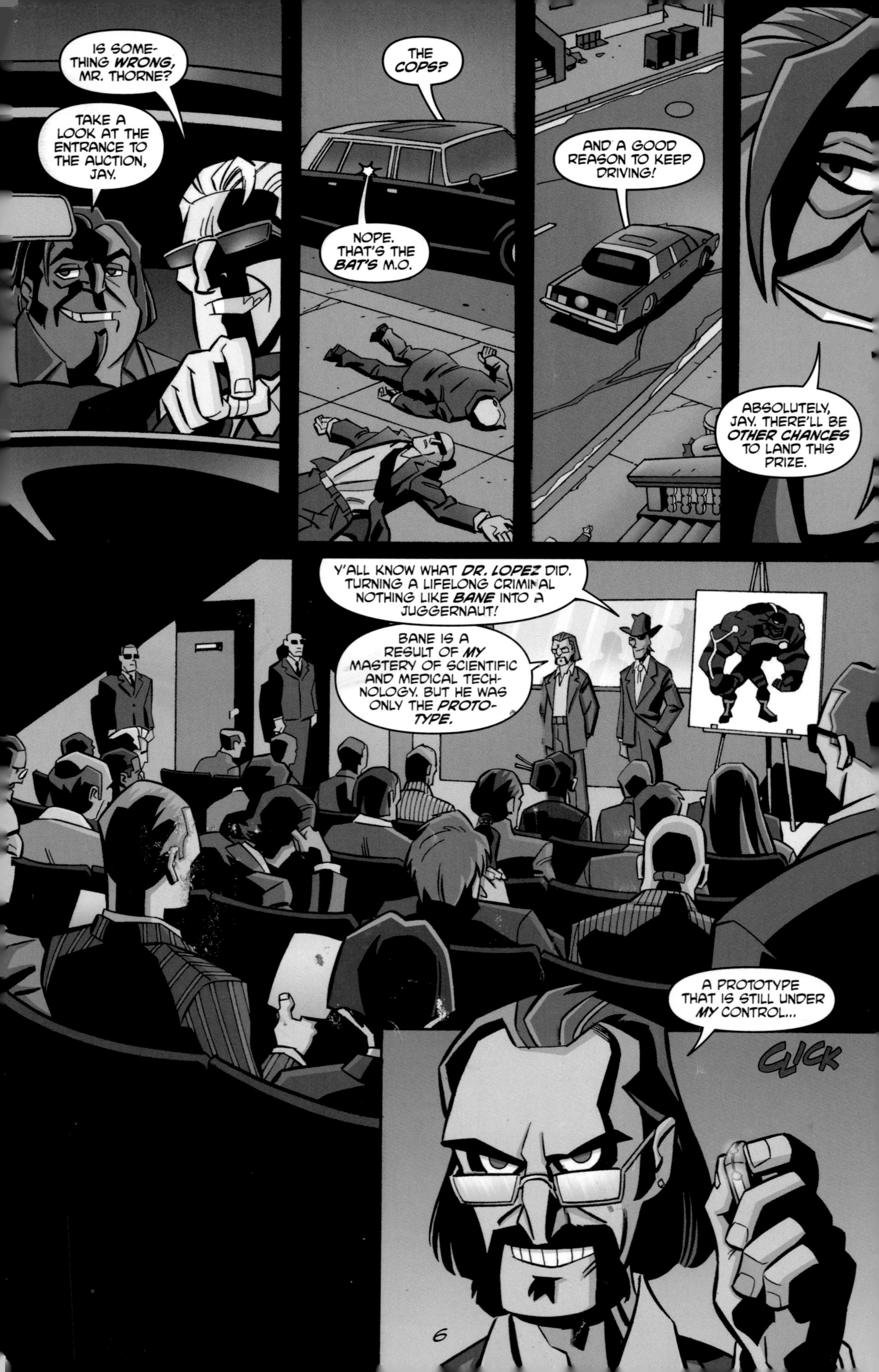
IS SOMETHING WRONG, MR. THORNE?
TAKE A LOOK AT THE ENTRANCE TO THE AUCTION, JAY.
THE COPS?
NOPE. THAT'S THE BAT'S M.O.
AND A GOOD REASON TO KEEP DRIVING!
ABSOLUTELY, JAY. THERE'LL BE OTHER CHANCES TO LAND THIS PRIZE.
Y'ALL KNOW WHAT DR. LOPEZ DID. TURNING A LIFELONG CRIMINAL NOTHING LIKE BANE INTO A JUGGERNAUT!
BANE IS A RESULT OF MY MASTERY OF SCIENTIFIC AND MEDICAL TECHNOLOGY. BUT HE WAS ONLY THE PROTOTYPE.
A PROTOTYPE THAT IS STILL UNDER MY CONTROL...
CLICK

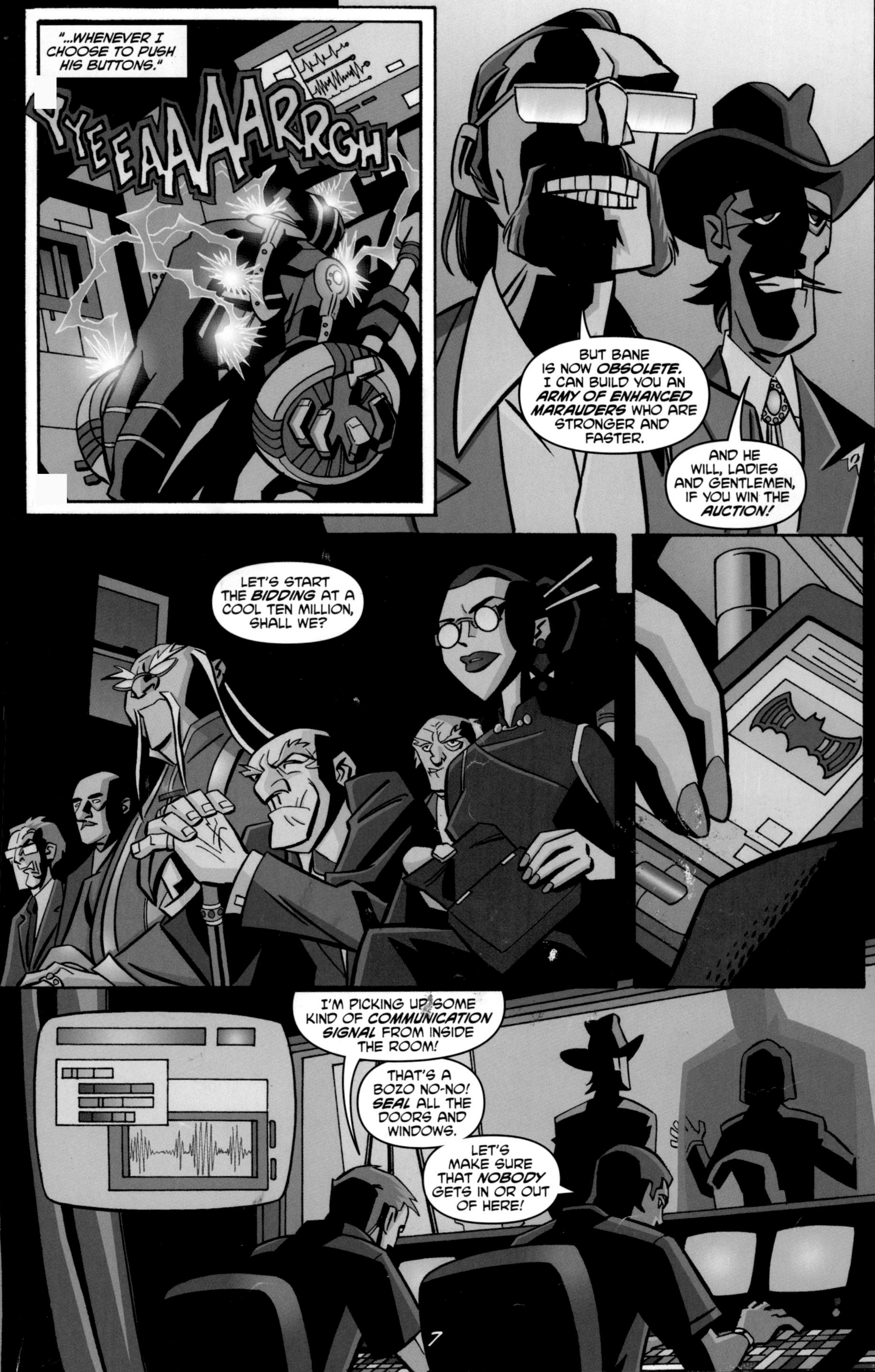
"...WHENEVER I CHOOSE TO PUSH HIS BUTTONS."
YYEEAAAARRRGH
BUT BANE IS NOW OBSOLETE. I CAN BUILD YOU AN ARMY OF ENHANCED MARAUDERS WHO ARE STRONGER AND FASTER.
AND HE WILL, LADIES AND GENTLEMEN, IF YOU WIN THE AUCTION!
LET'S START THE BIDDING AT A COOL TEN MILLION, SHALL WE?
I'M PICKING UP SOME KIND OF COMMUNICATION SIGNAL FROM INSIDE THE ROOM!
THAT'S A BOZO NO-NO! SEAL ALL THE DOORS AND WINDOWS.
LET'S MAKE SURE THAT NOBODY GETS IN OR OUT OF HERE!

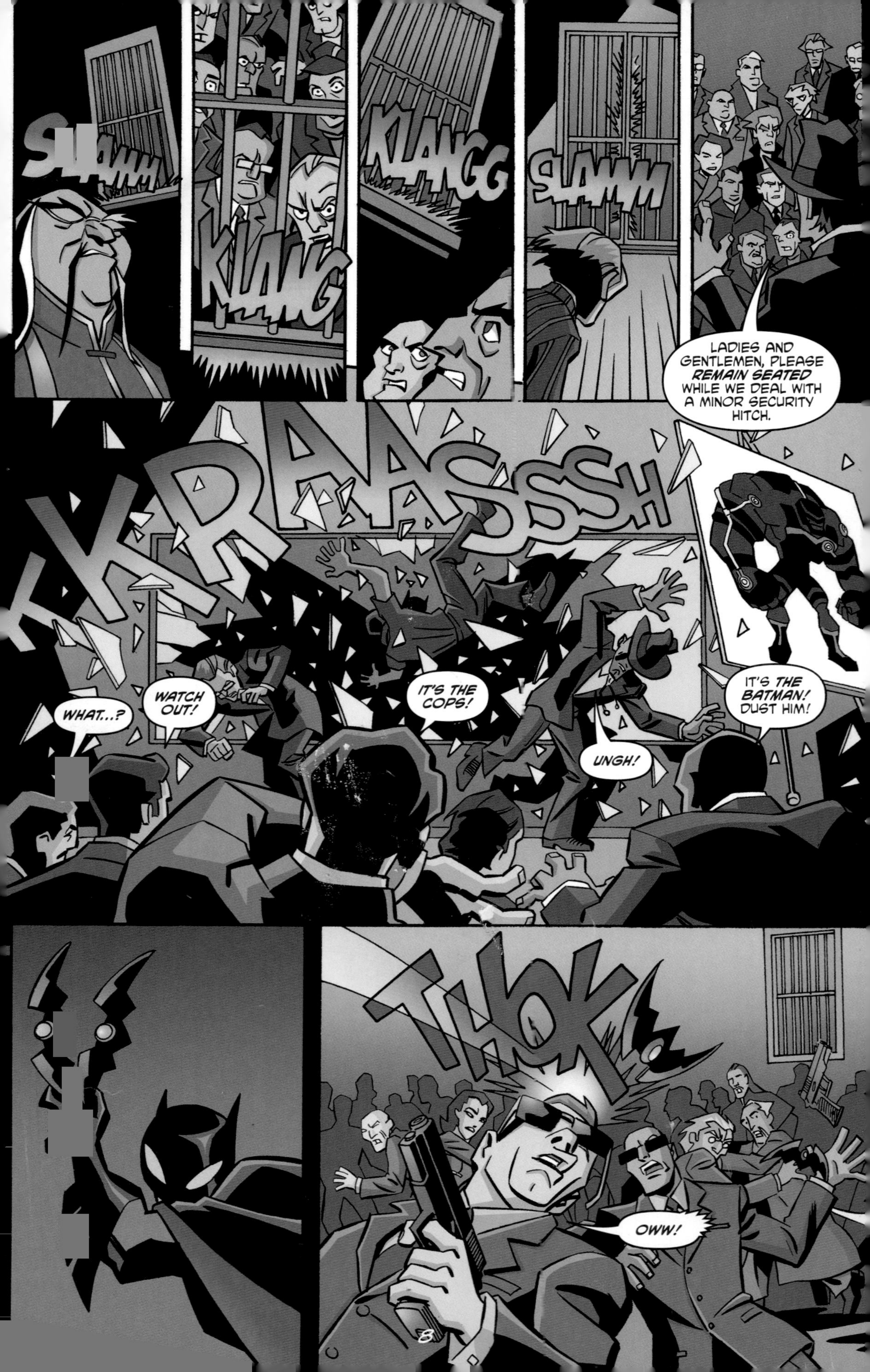
KLANG
KLANGG
SLAMM
LADIES AND GENTLEMEN, PLEASE *REMAIN SEATED* WHILE WE DEAL WITH A MINOR SECURITY HITCH.
KRAASSSH
WHAT...?
WATCH OUT!
IT'S THE COPS!
UNGH!
IT'S *THE BATMAN!* DUST HIM!
THOK
OWW!

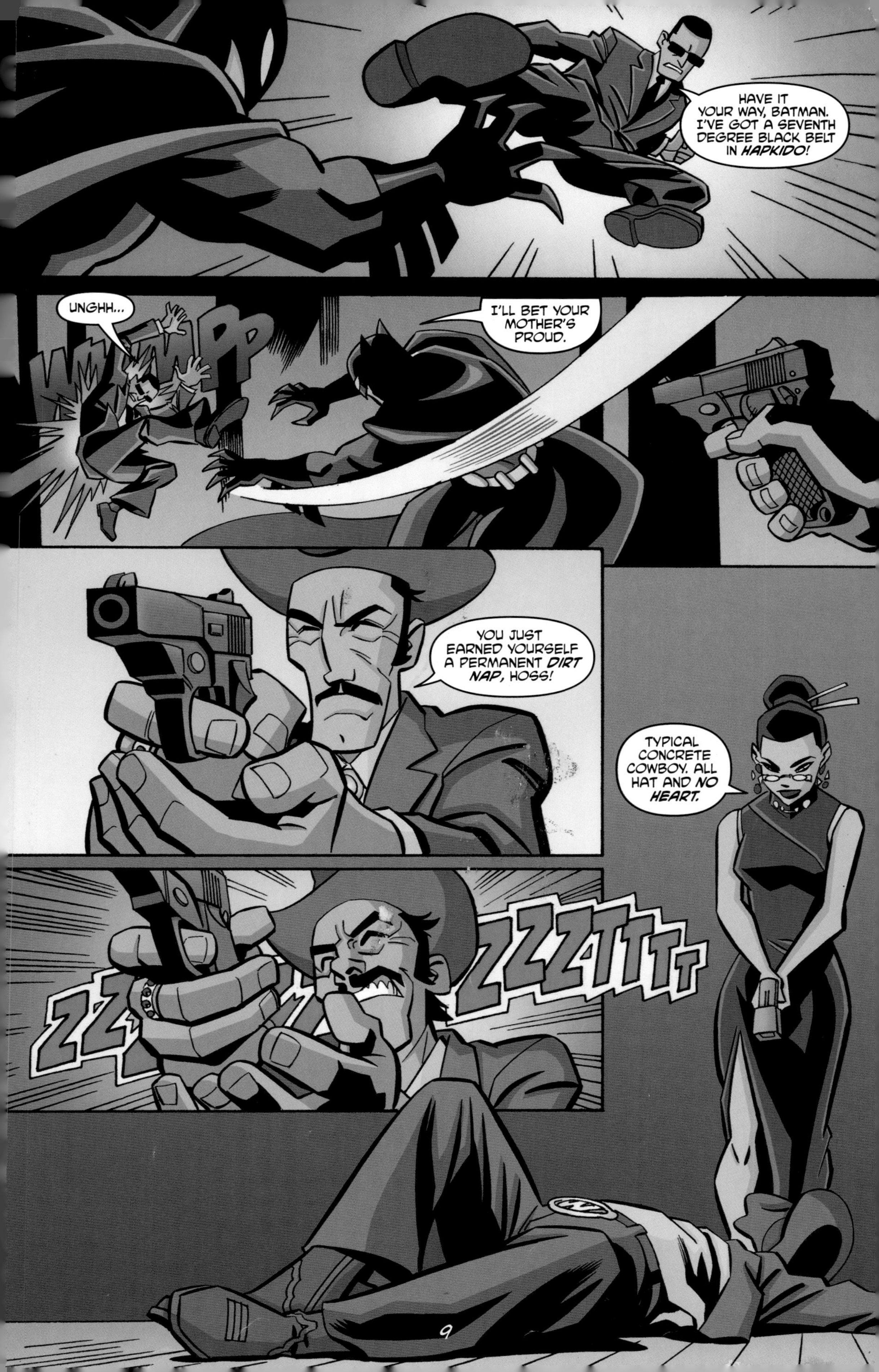
HAVE IT YOUR WAY, BATMAN. I'VE GOT A SEVENTH DEGREE BLACK BELT IN *HAPKIDO!*
UNGHH...
WHAMPP
I'LL BET YOUR MOTHER'S PROUD.
YOU JUST EARNED YOURSELF A PERMANENT *DIRT NAP,* HOSS!
TYPICAL CONCRETE COWBOY. ALL HAT AND *NO HEART.*
ZZZZZTTTT

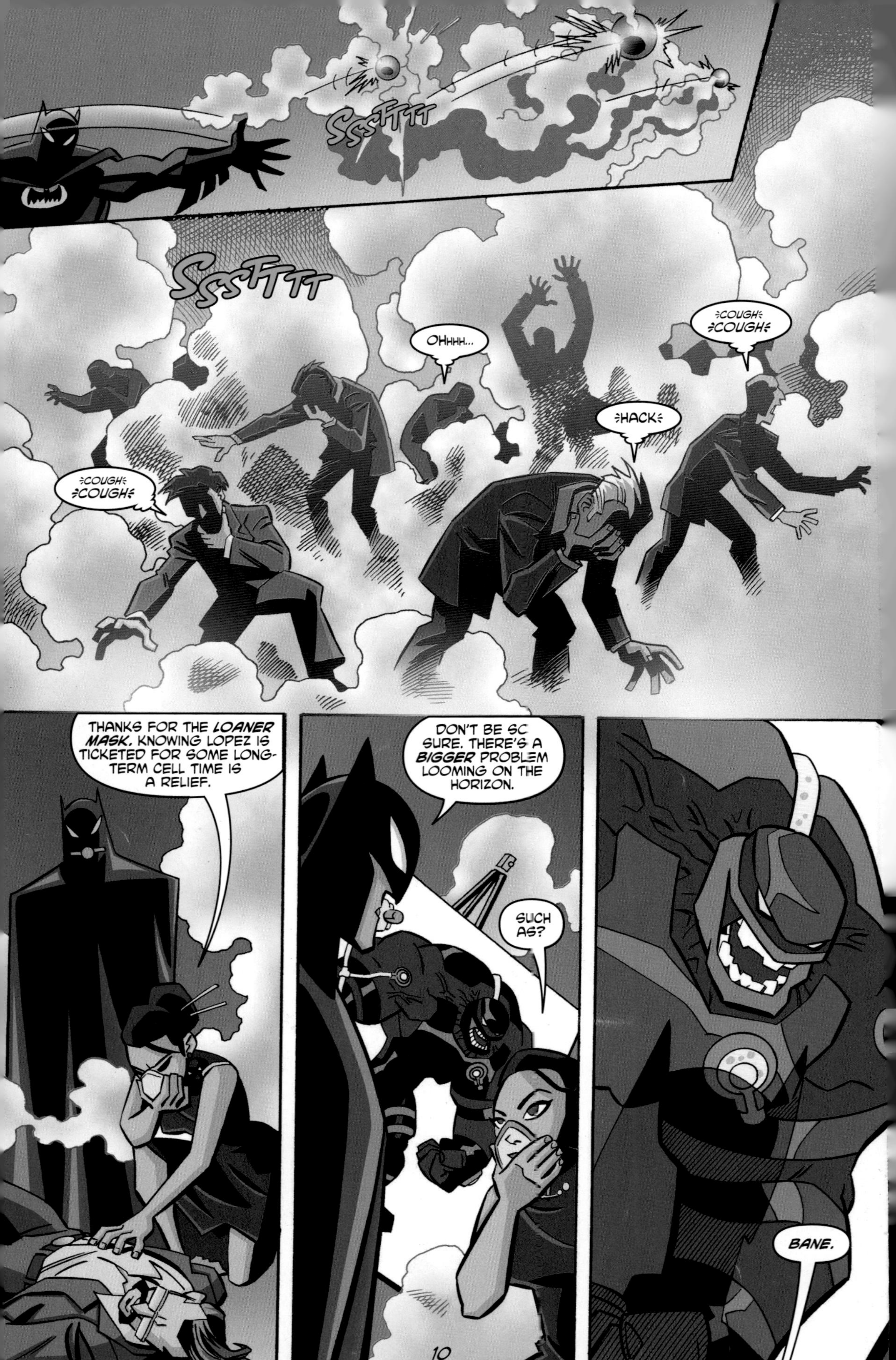
SSSTTTT
SSSTTTT
OHHHH...
COUGH COUGH
HACK
COUGH COUGH
THANKS FOR THE LOANER MASK. KNOWING LOPEZ IS TICKETED FOR SOME LONG-TERM CELL TIME IS A RELIEF.
DON'T BE SC SURE. THERE'S A BIGGER PROBLEM LOOMING ON THE HORIZON.
SUCH AS?
BANE.

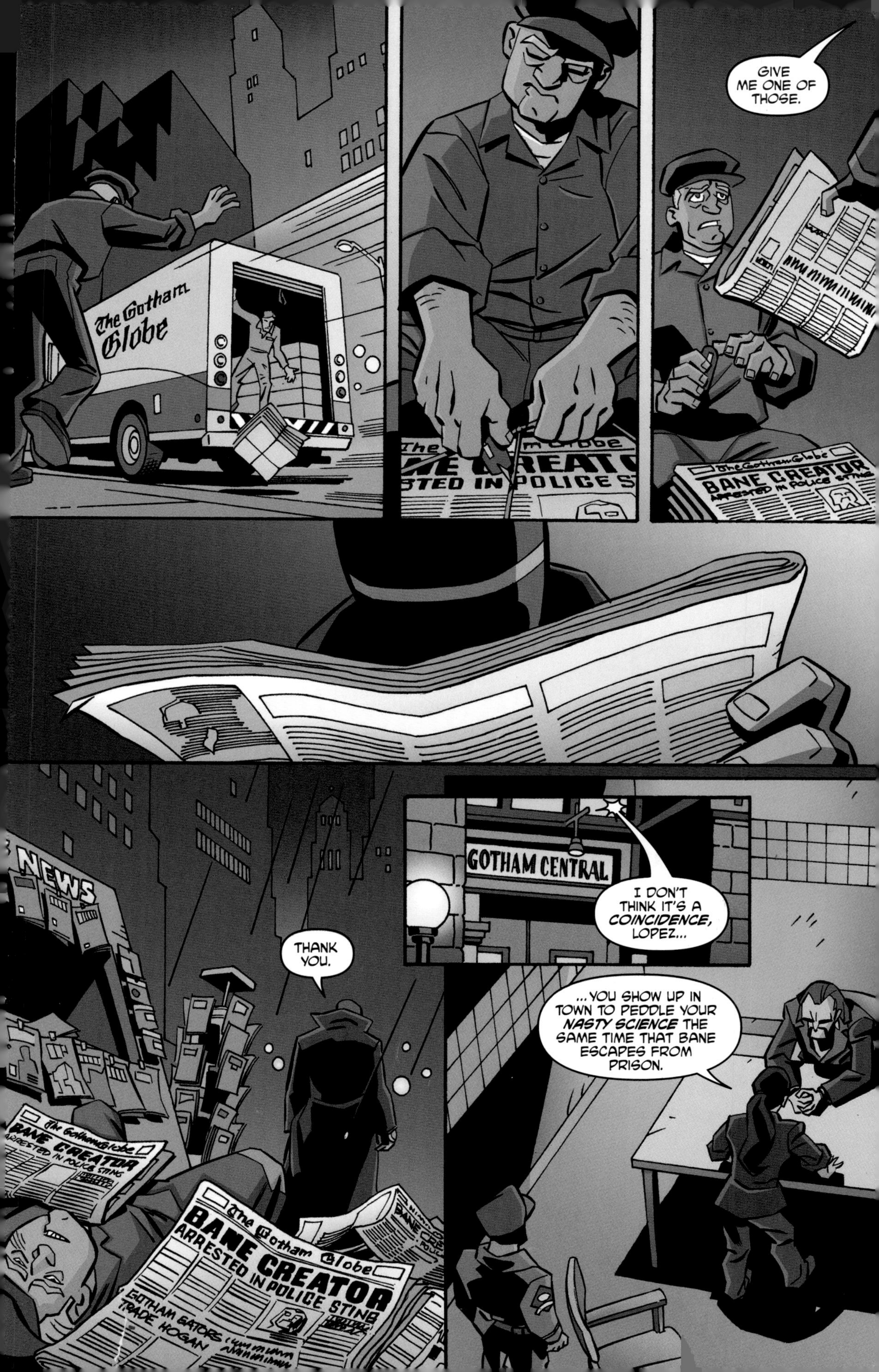
The Gotham Globe
GIVE ME ONE OF THOSE.
The Gotham Globe
BANE CREATOR
ARRESTED IN POLICE STING
NEWS
THANK YOU.
The Gotham Globe
BANE CREATOR
ARRESTED IN POLICE STING
GOTHAM GATORS TRADE HOGAN
GOTHAM CENTRAL
I DON'T THINK IT'S A *COINCIDENCE,* LOPEZ...
...YOU SHOW UP IN TOWN TO PEDDLE YOUR *NASTY SCIENCE* THE SAME TIME THAT BANE ESCAPES FROM PRISON.

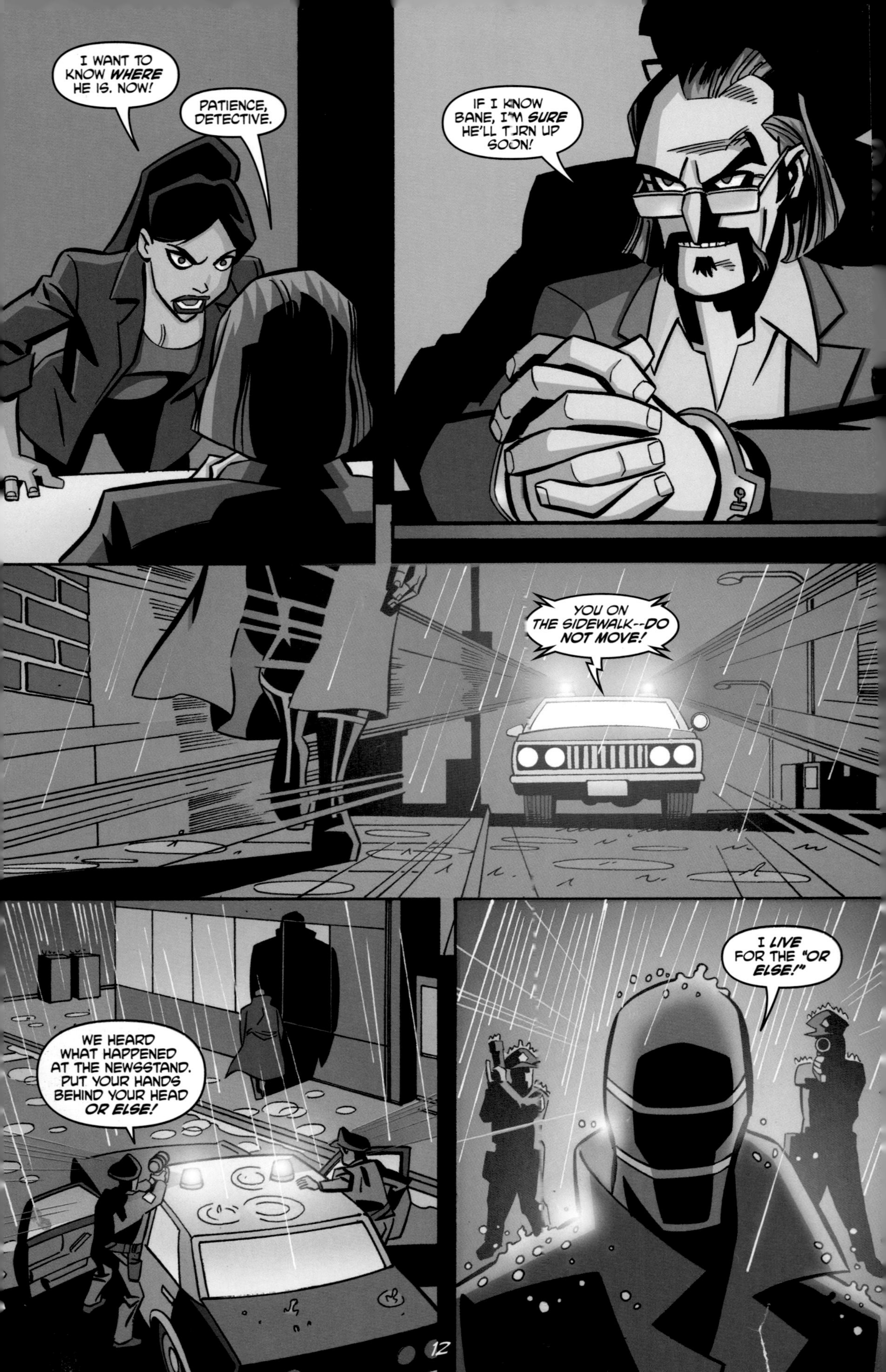
I WANT TO KNOW WHERE HE IS. NOW!
PATIENCE, DETECTIVE.
IF I KNOW BANE, I'M SURE HE'LL TURN UP SOON!
YOU ON THE SIDEWALK--DO NOT MOVE!
WE HEARD WHAT HAPPENED AT THE NEWSSTAND. PUT YOUR HANDS BEHIND YOUR HEAD OR ELSE!
I LIVE FOR THE "OR ELSE!"

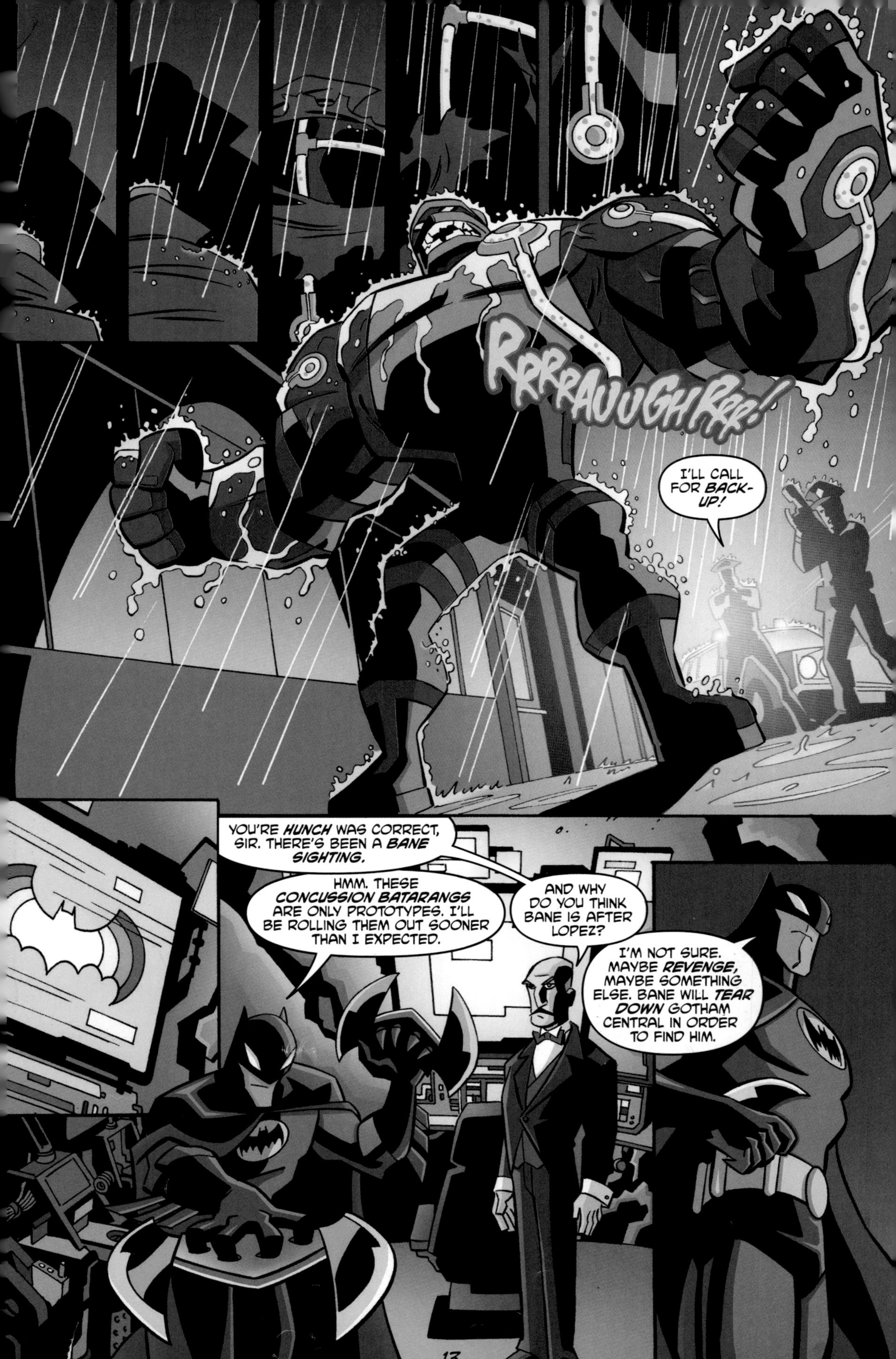
RRRRAUUUGHRRR!
I'LL CALL FOR BACK-UP!
YOU'RE HUNCH WAS CORRECT, SIR. THERE'S BEEN A BANE SIGHTING.
HMM. THESE CONCUSSION BATARANGS ARE ONLY PROTOTYPES. I'LL BE ROLLING THEM OUT SOONER THAN I EXPECTED.
AND WHY DO YOU THINK BANE IS AFTER LOPEZ?
I'M NOT SURE. MAYBE REVENGE, MAYBE SOMETHING ELSE. BANE WILL TEAR DOWN GOTHAM CENTRAL IN ORDER TO FIND HIM.

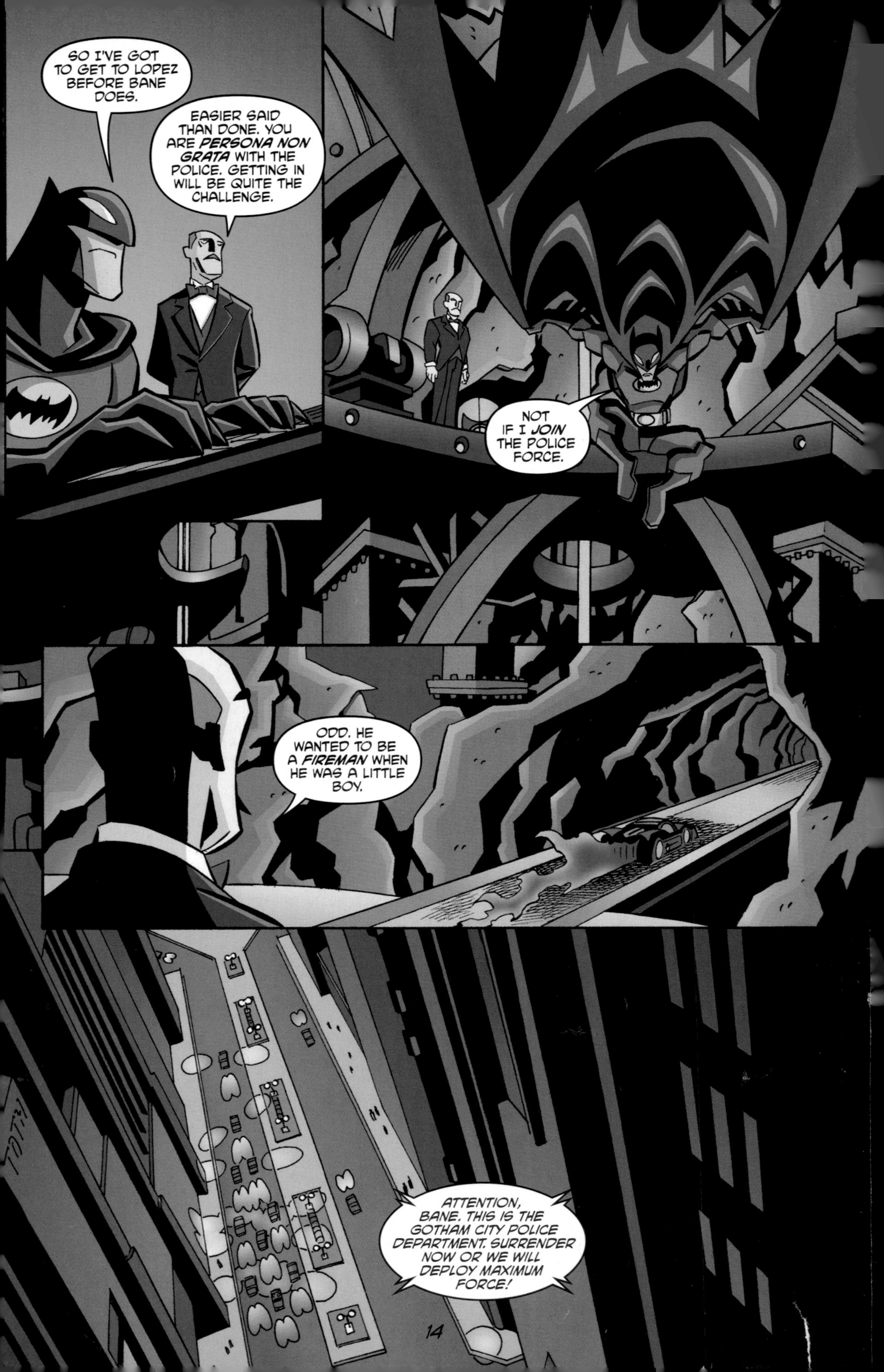
SO I'VE GOT TO GET TO LOPEZ BEFORE BANE DOES.
EASIER SAID THAN DONE. YOU ARE PERSONA NON GRATA WITH THE POLICE. GETTING IN WILL BE QUITE THE CHALLENGE.
NOT IF I JOIN THE POLICE FORCE.
ODD. HE WANTED TO BE A FIREMAN WHEN HE WAS A LITTLE BOY.
ATTENTION, BANE. THIS IS THE GOTHAM CITY POLICE DEPARTMENT. SURRENDER NOW OR WE WILL DEPLOY MAXIMUM FORCE!

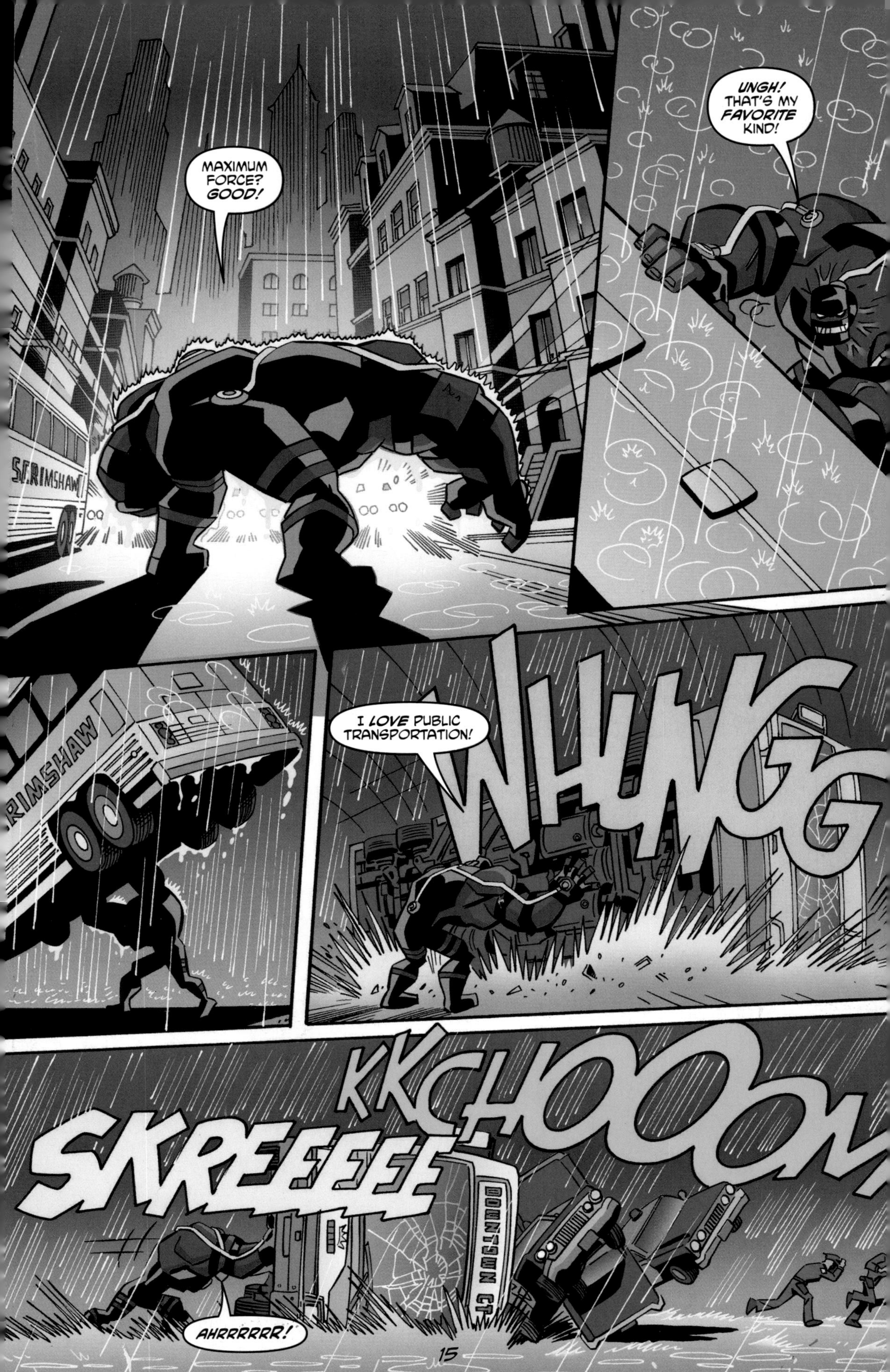
MAXIMUM FORCE? GOOD!
SCRIMSHAW
UNGH! THAT'S MY FAVORITE KIND!
SCRIMSHAW
I LOVE PUBLIC TRANSPORTATION!
WHUNGG
KKCHOOOOM
SKREEEEEE
DOWNTOWN CT
AHRRRRRR!

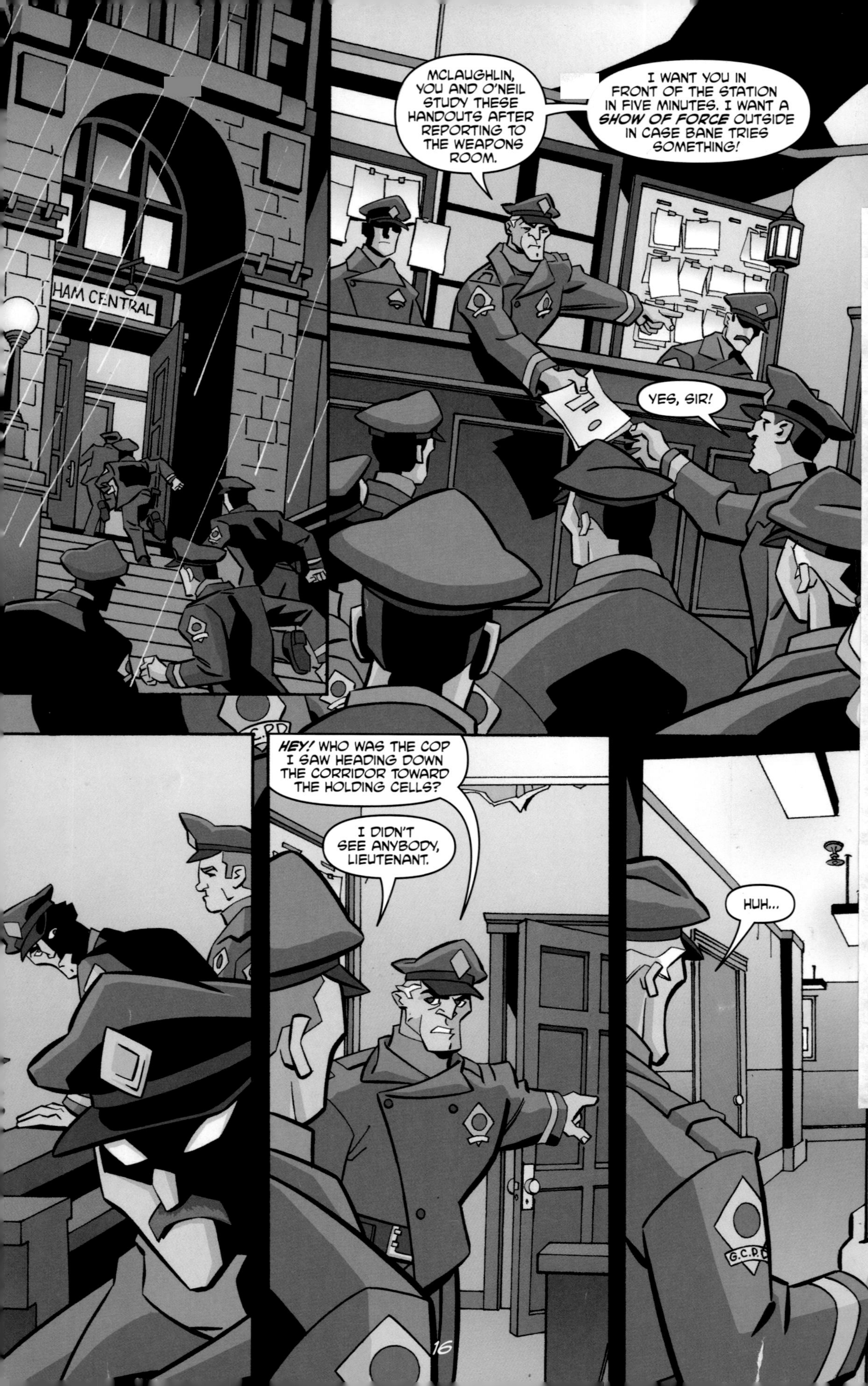
HAM CENTRAL
MCLAUGHLIN, YOU AND O'NEIL STUDY THESE HANDOUTS AFTER REPORTING TO THE WEAPONS ROOM.
I WANT YOU IN FRONT OF THE STATION IN FIVE MINUTES. I WANT A ***SHOW OF FORCE*** OUTSIDE IN CASE BANE TRIES SOMETHING!
YES, SIR!
HEY! WHO WAS THE COP I SAW HEADING DOWN THE CORRIDOR TOWARD THE HOLDING CELLS?
I DIDN'T SEE ANYBODY, LIEUTENANT.
HUH...

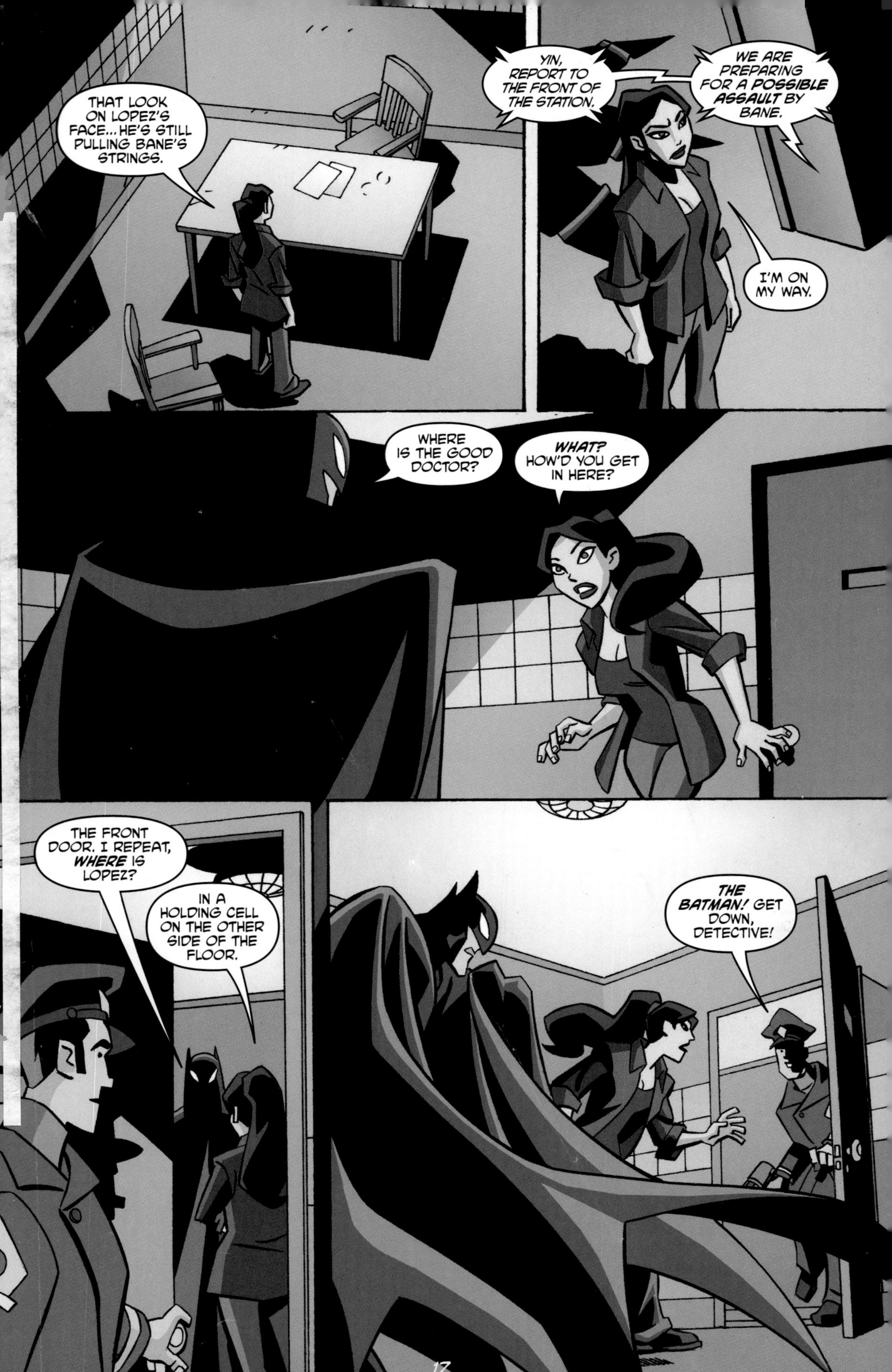

THAT LOOK ON LOPEZ'S FACE... HE'S STILL PULLING BANE'S STRINGS.
YIN, REPORT TO THE FRONT OF THE STATION.
WE ARE PREPARING FOR A POSSIBLE ASSAULT BY BANE.
I'M ON MY WAY.
WHERE IS THE GOOD DOCTOR?
WHAT? HOW'D YOU GET IN HERE?
THE FRONT DOOR. I REPEAT, WHERE IS LOPEZ?
IN A HOLDING CELL ON THE OTHER SIDE OF THE FLOOR.
THE BATMAN! GET DOWN, DETECTIVE!

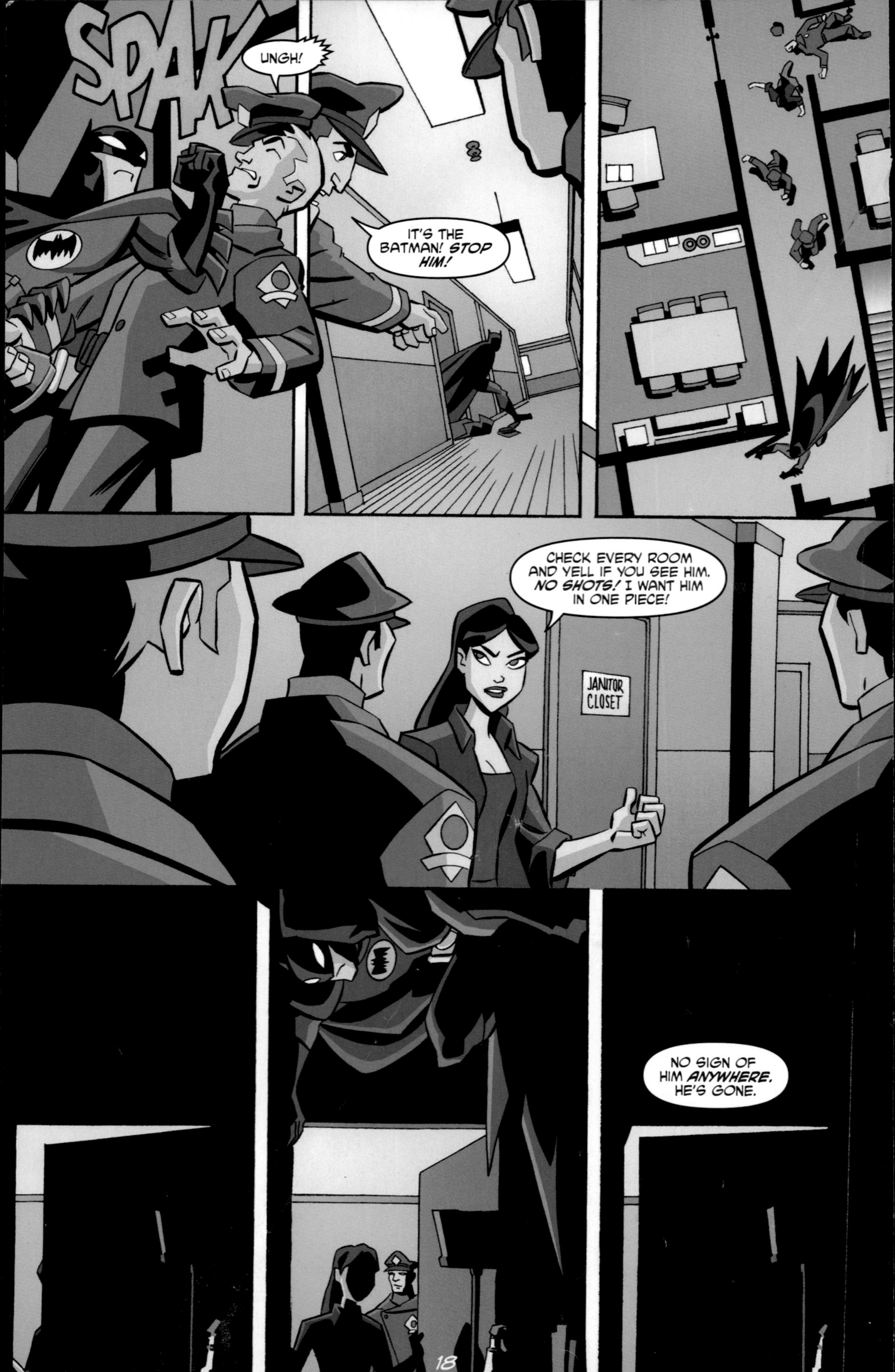
SPAK!
UNGH!
IT'S THE BATMAN! STOP HIM!
CHECK EVERY ROOM AND YELL IF YOU SEE HIM. NO SHOTS! I WANT HIM IN ONE PIECE!
JANITOR CLOSET
NO SIGN OF HIM ANYWHERE. HE'S GONE.

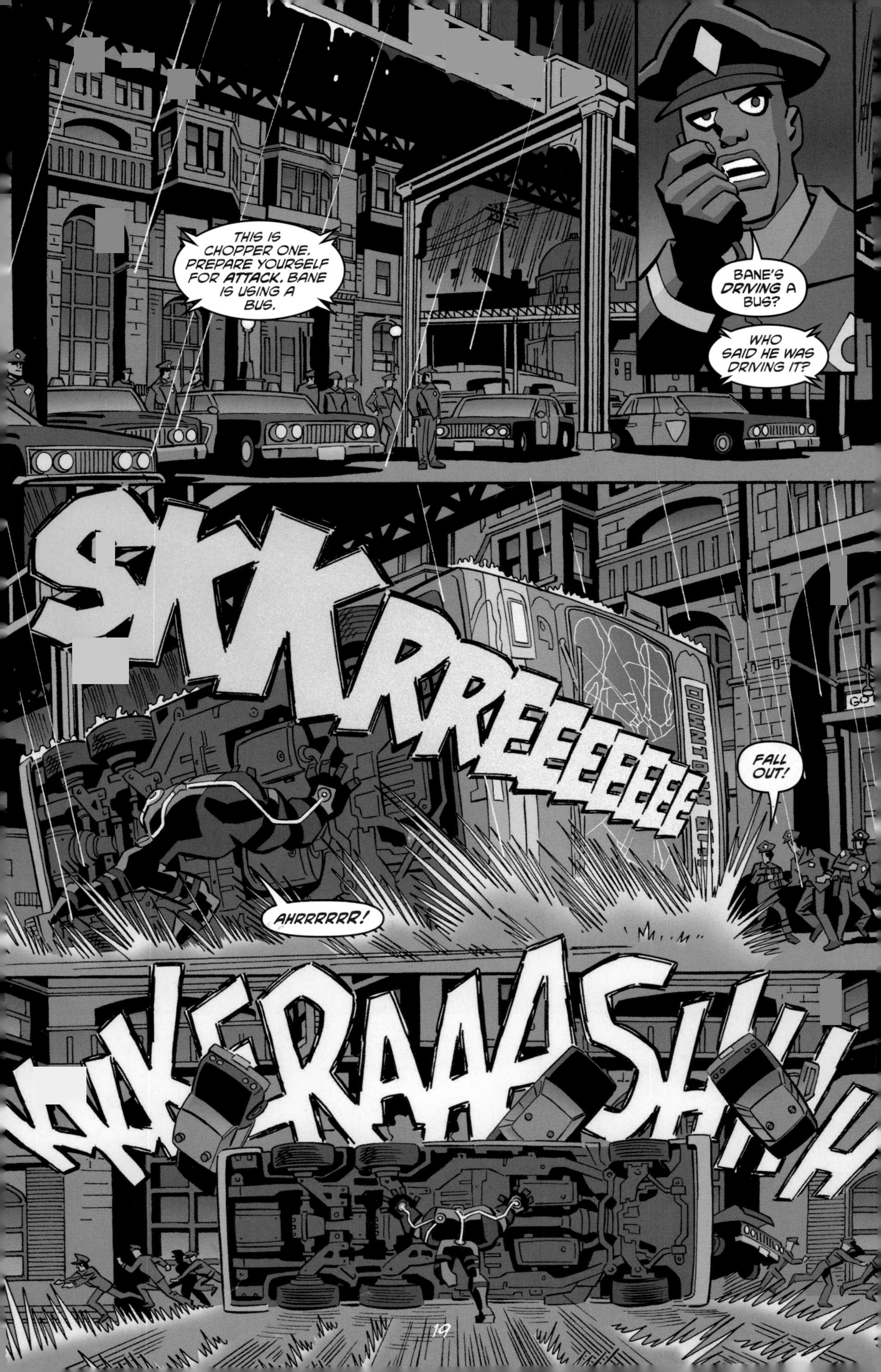
THIS IS CHOPPER ONE. PREPARE YOURSELF FOR ATTACK. BANE IS USING A BUS.
BANE'S DRIVING A BUS?
WHO SAID HE WAS DRIVING IT?
FALL OUT!
AHRRRRRR!

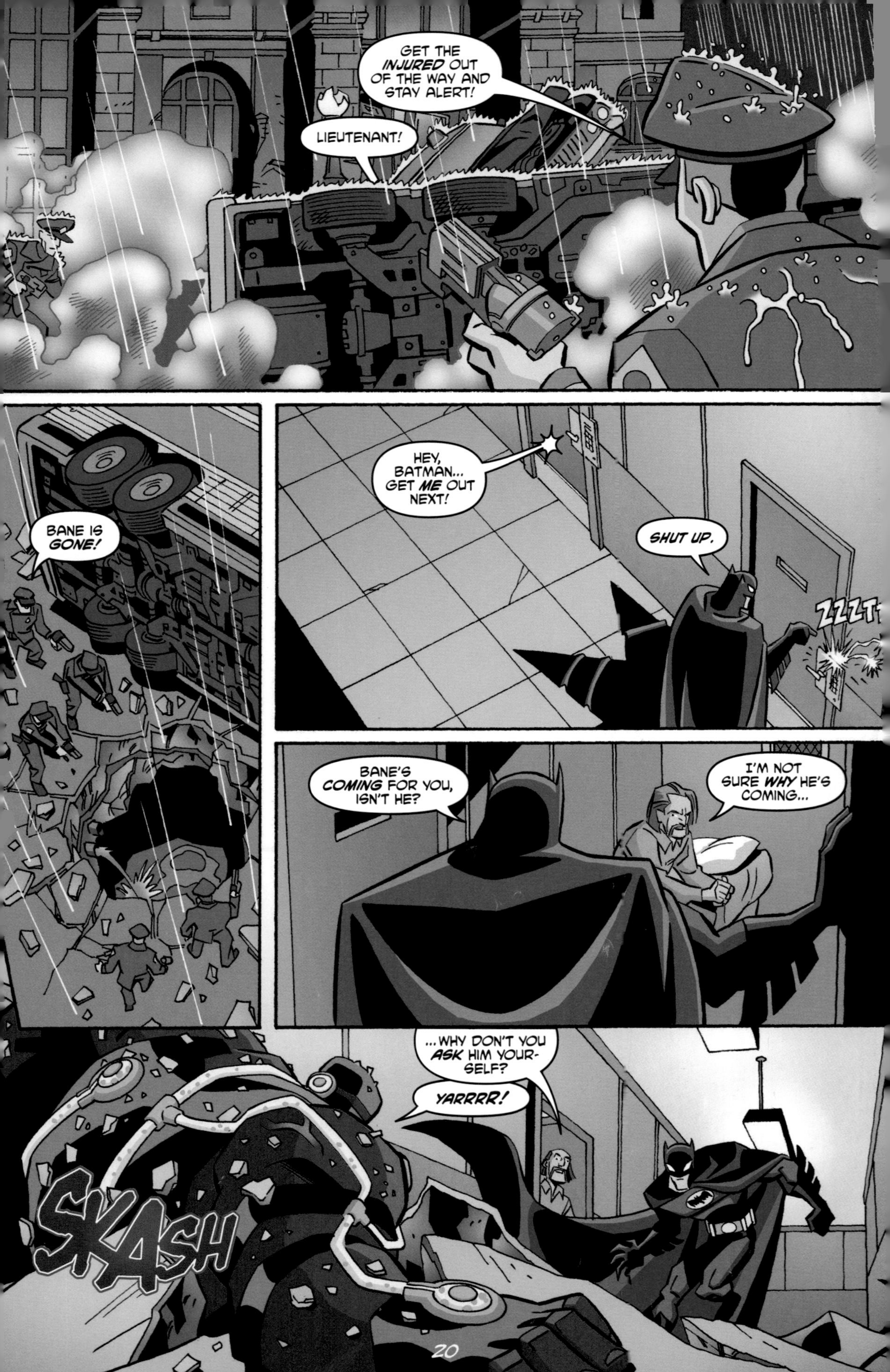
GET THE INJURED OUT OF THE WAY AND STAY ALERT!
LIEUTENANT!
BANE IS GONE!
HEY, BATMAN... GET ME OUT NEXT!
SHUT UP.
ZZZT
BANE'S COMING FOR YOU, ISN'T HE?
I'M NOT SURE WHY HE'S COMING...
...WHY DON'T YOU ASK HIM YOUR-SELF?
YARRRR!
SKASH

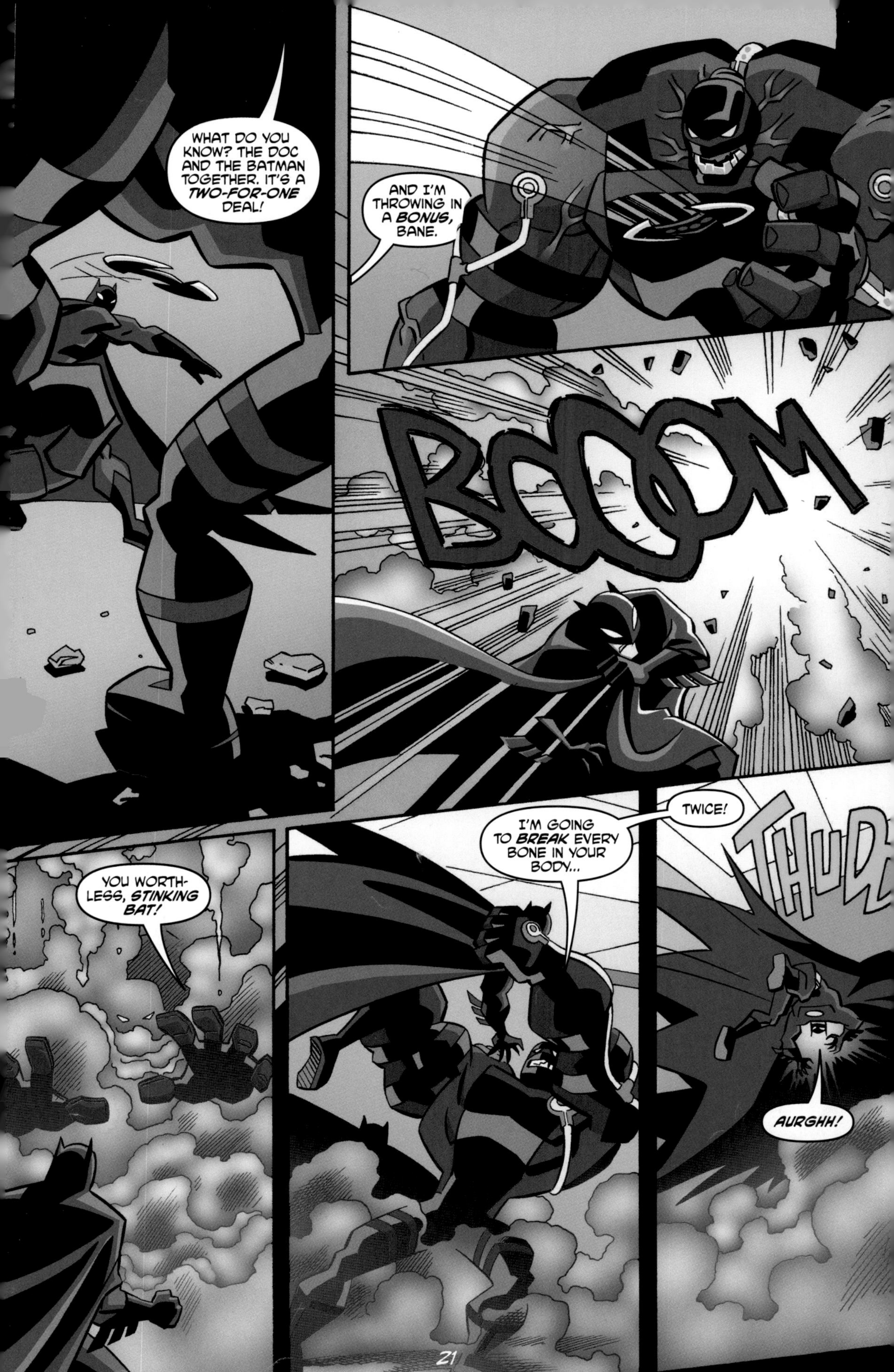
WHAT DO YOU KNOW? THE DOC AND THE BATMAN TOGETHER. IT'S A TWO-FOR-ONE DEAL!
AND I'M THROWING IN A BONUS, BANE.
BOOOM
YOU WORTH-LESS, STINKING BAT!
I'M GOING TO BREAK EVERY BONE IN YOUR BODY...
TWICE!
THUD
AURGHH!

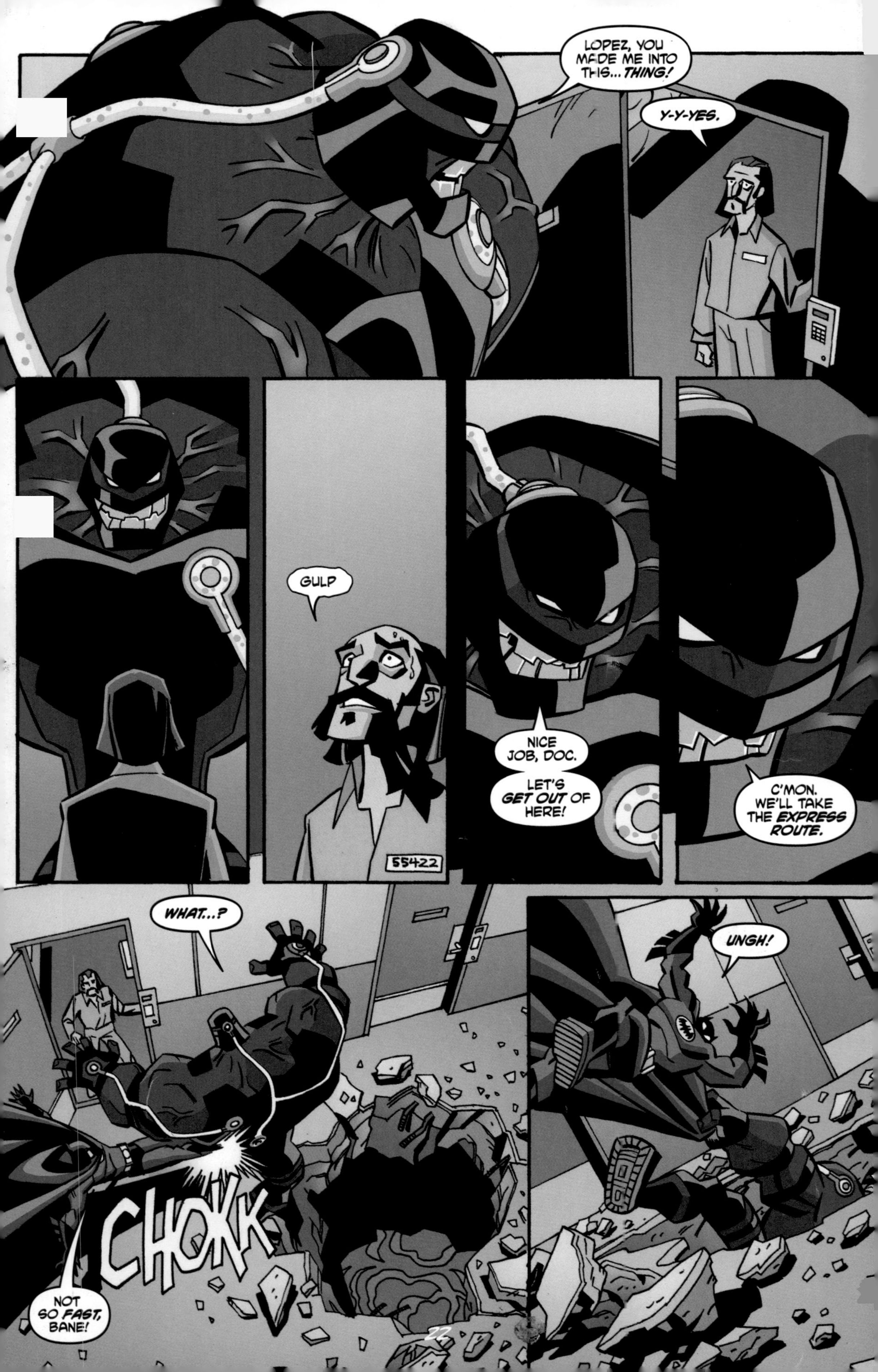
LOPEZ, YOU MADE ME INTO THIS... THING!
Y-Y-YES.
GULP
55422
NICE JOB, DOC.
LET'S GET OUT OF HERE!
C'MON. WE'LL TAKE THE EXPRESS ROUTE.
WHAT...?
CHOKK
NOT SO FAST, BANE!
UNGH!

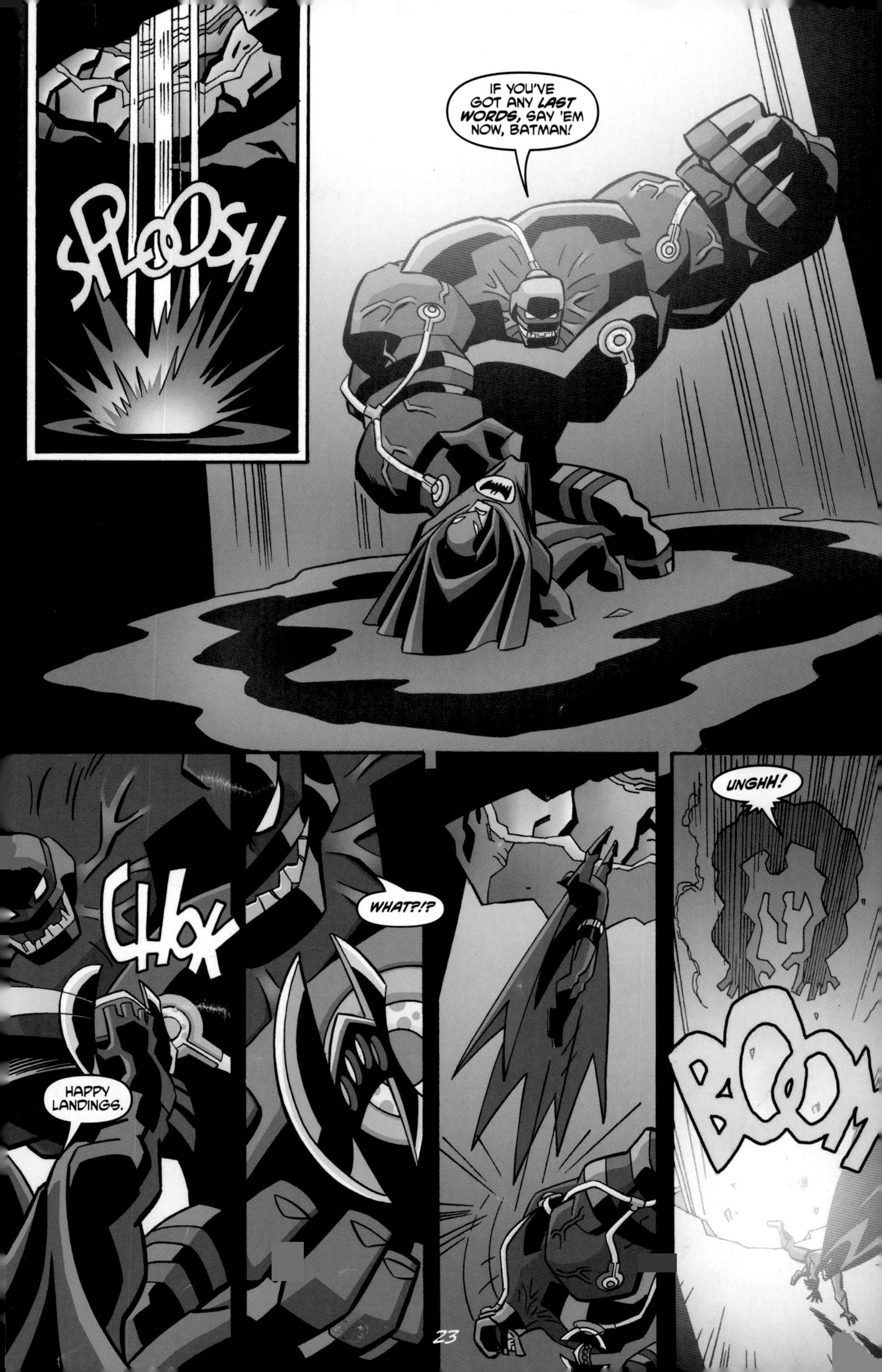

SPLOOSH
IF YOU'VE GOT ANY *LAST WORDS*, SAY 'EM NOW, BATMAN!
CHOK
HAPPY LANDINGS.
WHAT?!?
UNGHH!
BOOM

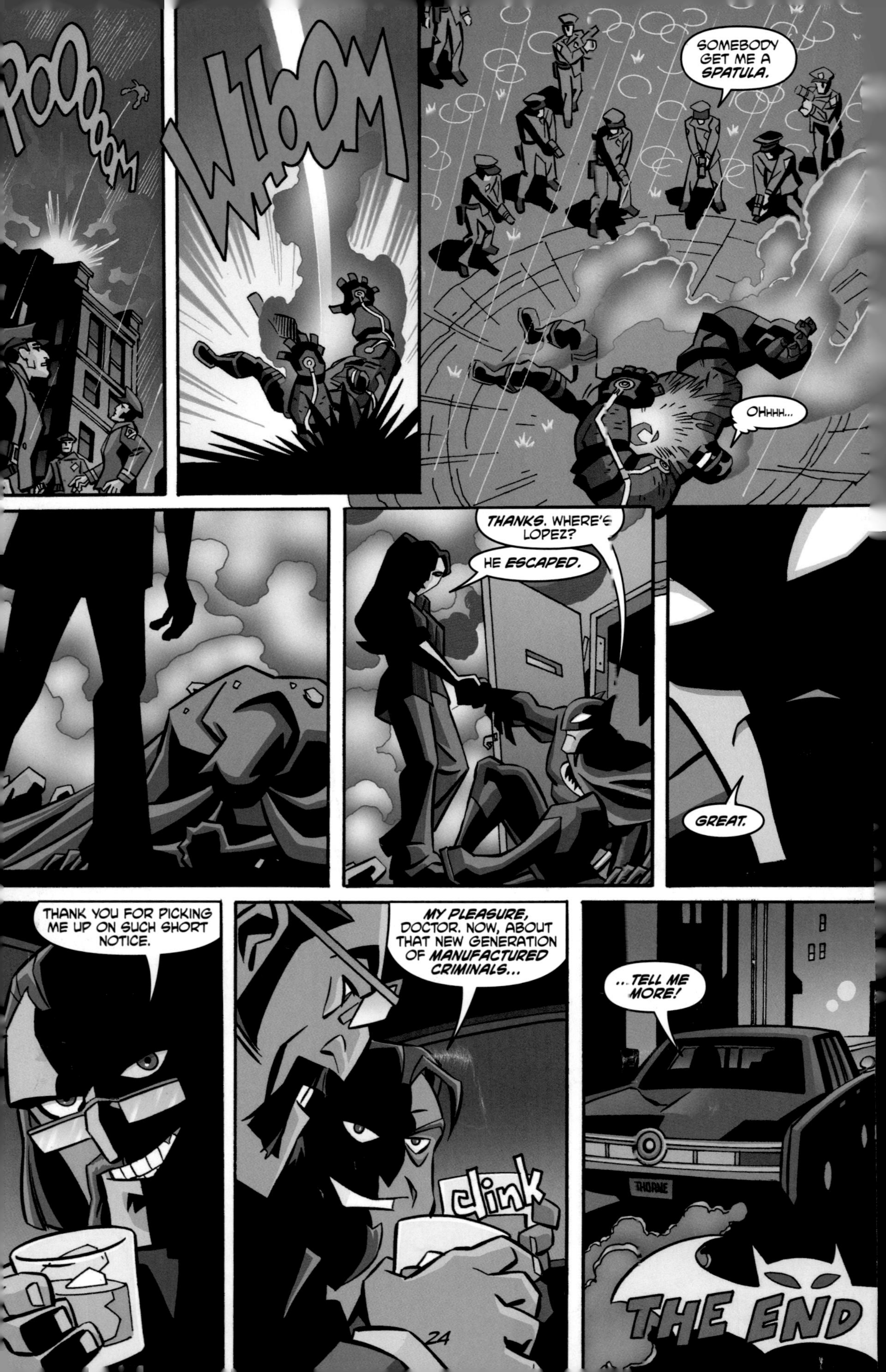
POOOoOOM
WHOOM
SOMEBODY GET ME A SPATULA.
OHHHH...
THANKS. WHERE'S LOPEZ?
HE ESCAPED.
GREAT.
THANK YOU FOR PICKING ME UP ON SUCH SHORT NOTICE.
MY PLEASURE, DOCTOR. NOW, ABOUT THAT NEW GENERATION OF MANUFACTURED CRIMINALS...
clink
...TELL ME MORE!
THORNE
THE END

CREATORS

BILL MATHENY WRITER
Along with comics like THE BATMAN STRIKES, Bill Matheny has written for TV series including KRYPTO THE SUPERDOG, WHERE'S WALDO, A PUP NAMED SCOOBY-DOO, and many others.

CHRISTOPHER JONES PENCILLER
Christopher Jones is an artist who has worked for DC Comics, Image, Malibu, Caliber, and Sundragon Comics.

TERRY BEATTY INKER
Terry Beatty has inked THE BATMAN STRIKES! and BATMAN: THE BRAVE AND THE BOLD as well as several other DC Comics graphic novels.

GLOSSARY

clearance (KLEER-uhnss)--permission to do something

coincidence (koh-IN-si-duhnss)--a surprising event that seems to happen by chance

concussion (kuhn-KUHSH-uhn)--an injury to the brain

deploy (di-PLOY)--to move or put into position

enhanced (en-HANST)--made something bigger or better

hapkido (hahp-KEE-doh)--a Korean martial art

hunch (HUHNCH)--an idea that is based on a feeling rather than fact

obsolete (ahb-suh-LEET)--no longer in use

persona non grata (per-SOH-nah nahn GRAT-uh)--an unwelcome person

prototype (PROH-tuh-tipe)--the first version of an invention used to test an idea

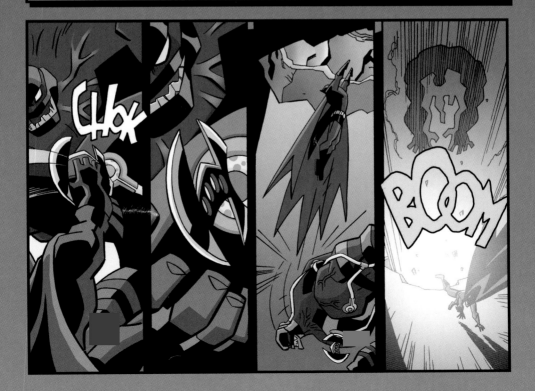

VISUAL QUESTIONS & PROMPTS

1. How do the artists let us know that there's a search going on for Bane in this panel? What are some other ways they could have depicted the search?

ATTENTION, BANE. THIS IS THE GOTHAM CITY POLICE DEPARTMENT. SURRENDER NOW OR WE WILL DEPLOY MAXIMUM FORCE!

2. How do the shadows in these panels give the readers a clue as to what will happen next?

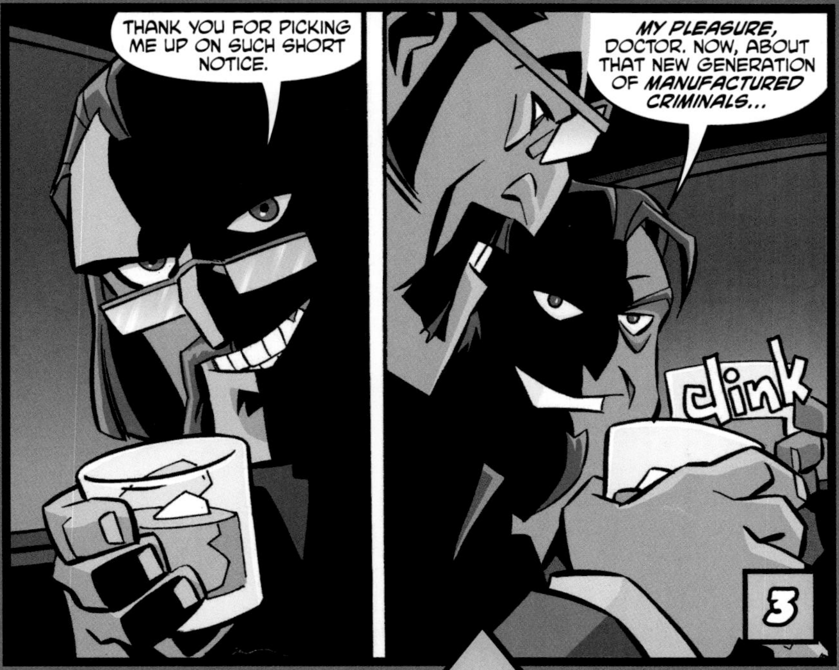
THANK YOU FOR PICKING ME UP ON SUCH SHORT NOTICE.
MY PLEASURE, DOCTOR. NOW, ABOUT THAT NEW GENERATION OF MANUFACTURED CRIMINALS...
clink
3

3. Why do you think the characters' faces are shadowed here? What does that effect have on the scene?

4. How would this scene be different if we were seeing it from Yin's perspective?

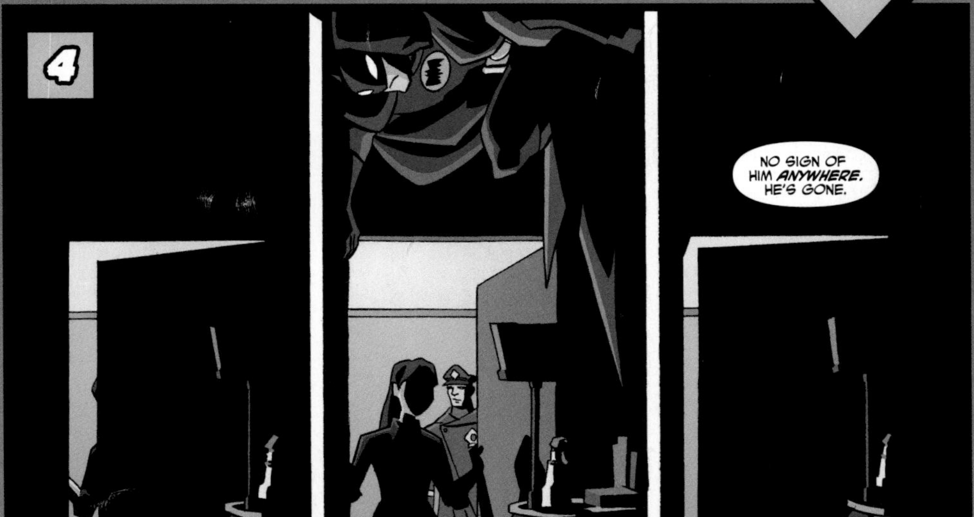
4
NO SIGN OF HIM ANYWHERE. HE'S GONE.

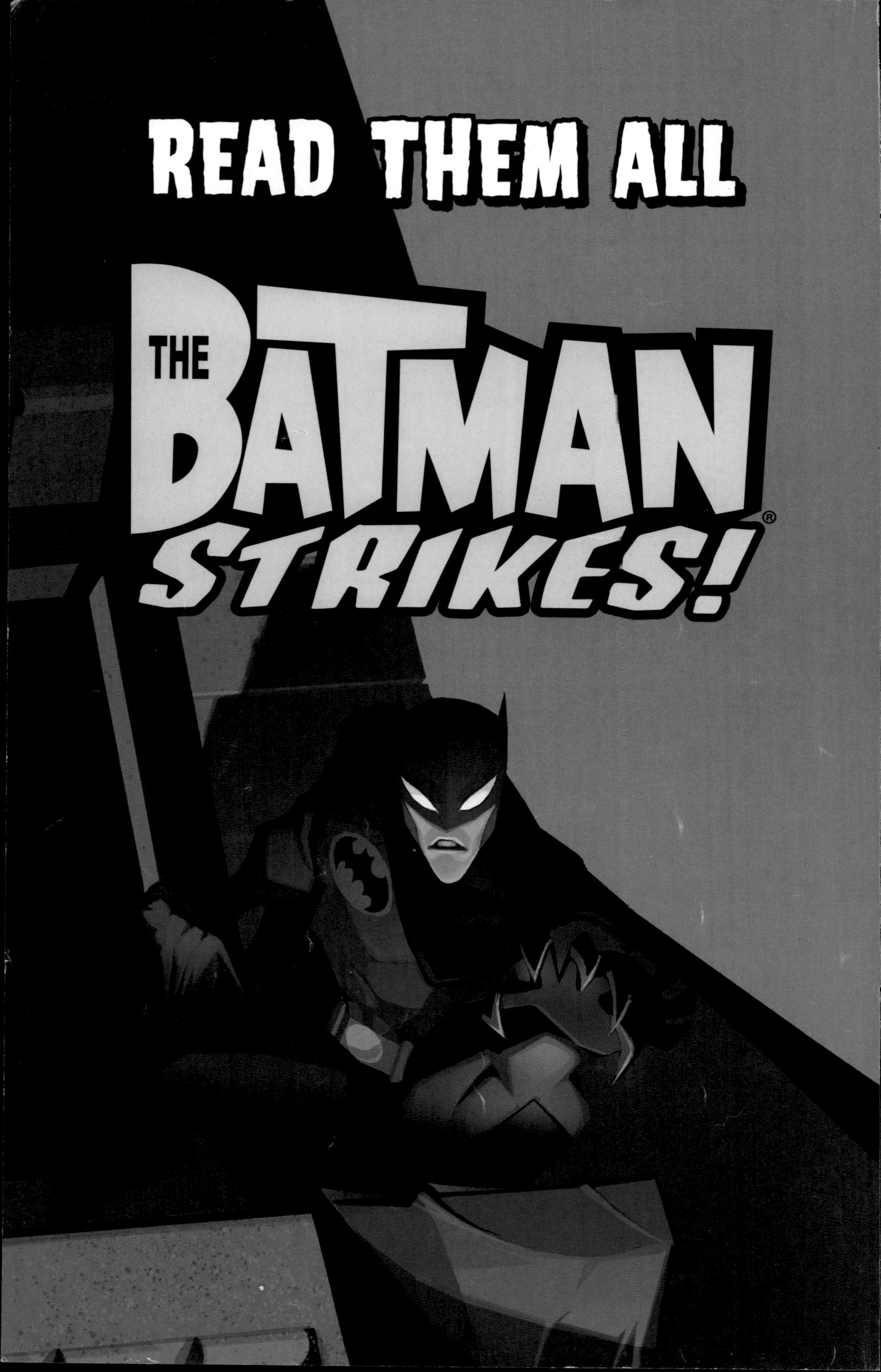
READ THEM ALL
THE BATMAN STRIKES!®

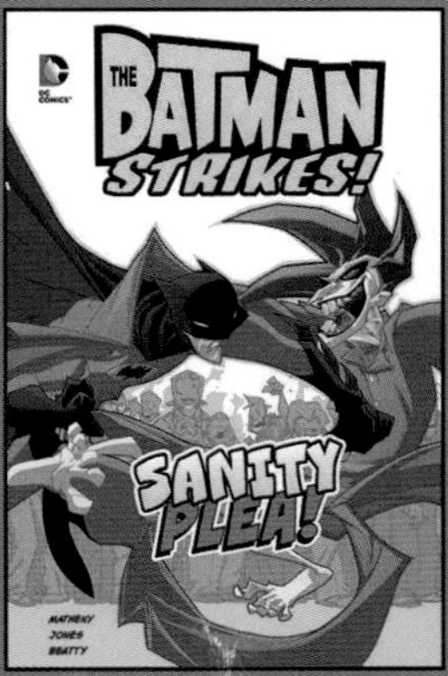
THE BATMAN STRIKES!
SANITY PLEA!
MATHENY
JONES
BEATTY

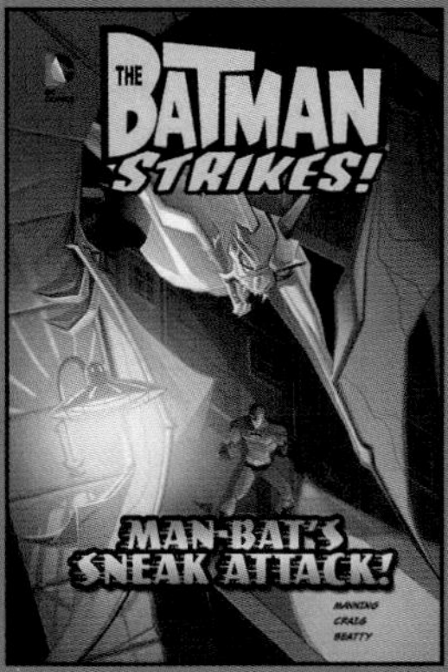
THE BATMAN STRIKES!
MAN-BAT'S SNEAK ATTACK!
MANNING
CRAIG
BEATTY

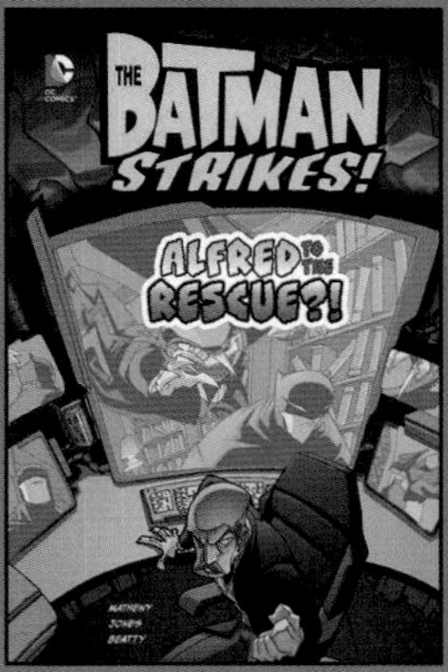
THE BATMAN STRIKES!
ALFRED TO THE RESCUE?!
MATHENY
JONES
BEATTY

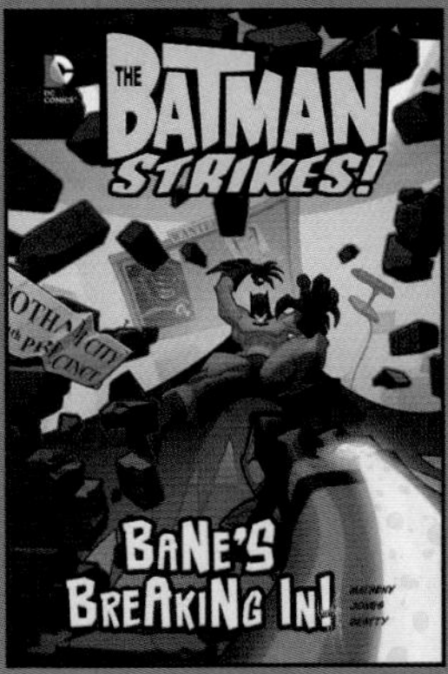
THE BATMAN STRIKES!
BANE'S BREAKING IN!
MATHENY
JONES
BEATTY

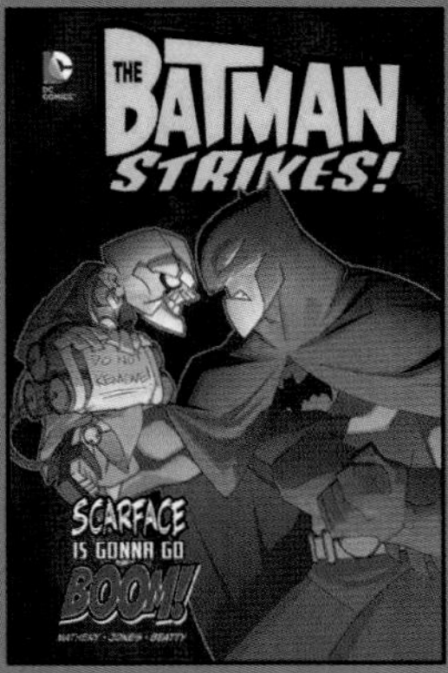
THE BATMAN STRIKES!
SCARFACE IS GONNA GO BOOM!
MATHENY · JONES · BEATTY

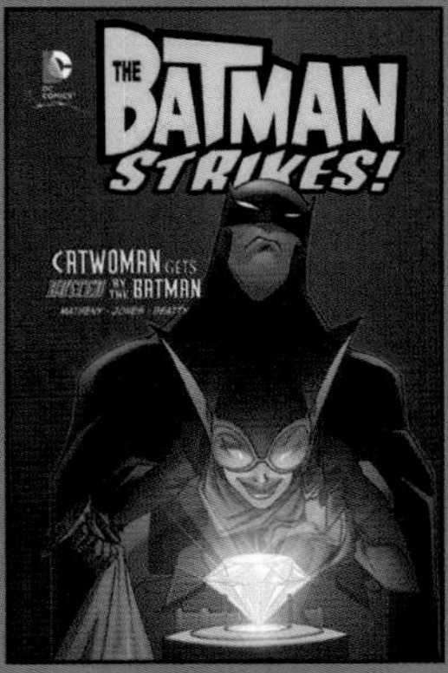
THE BATMAN STRIKES!
CATWOMAN GETS BUSTED BY THE BATMAN
MATHENY · JONES · BEATTY

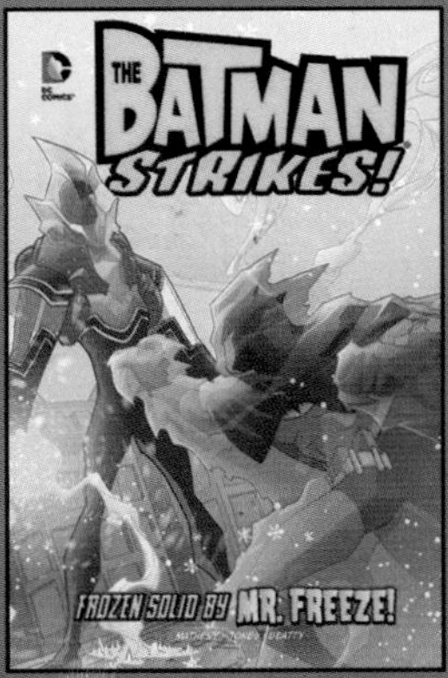
THE BATMAN STRIKES!
FROZEN SOLID BY MR. FREEZE!
MATHENY · JONES · BEATTY

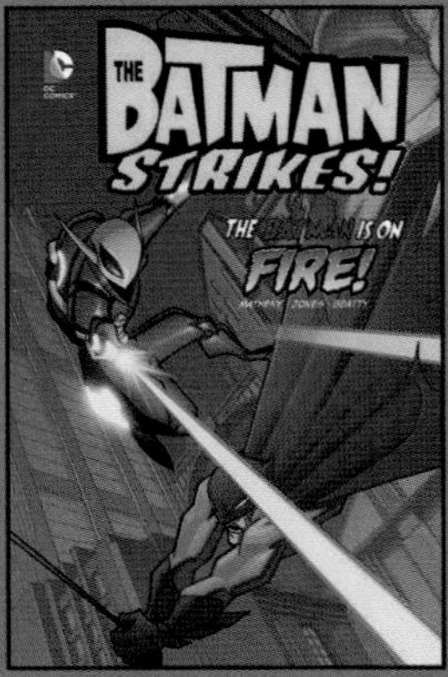
THE BATMAN STRIKES!
THE BATMAN IS ON FIRE!
MATHENY · JONES · BEATTY

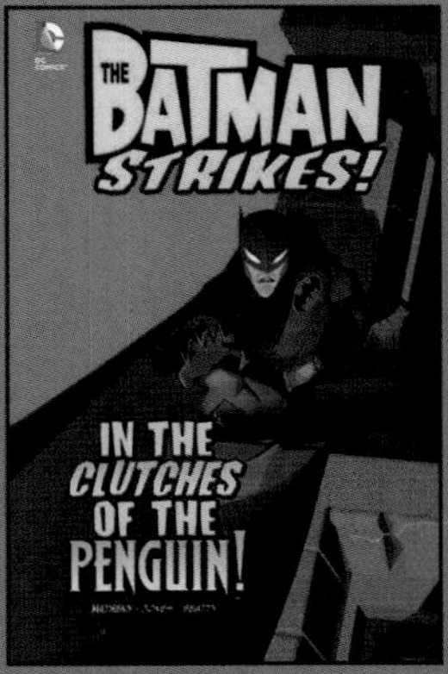
THE BATMAN STRIKES!
IN THE CLUTCHES OF THE PENGUIN!
MATHENY · JONES · BEATTY

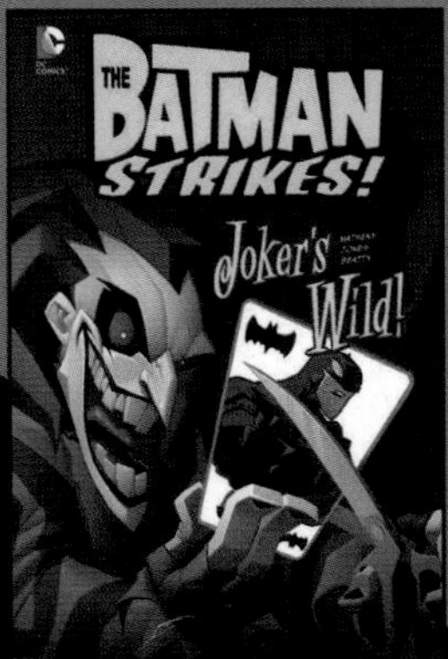
THE BATMAN STRIKES!
Joker's Wild!
MATHENY
JONES
BEATTY

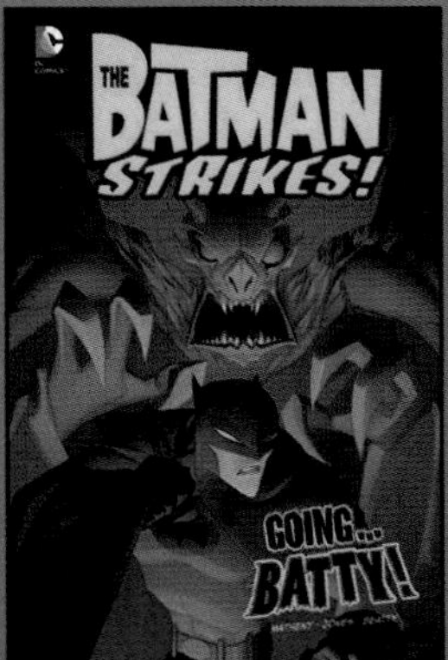
THE BATMAN STRIKES!
GOING... BATTY!

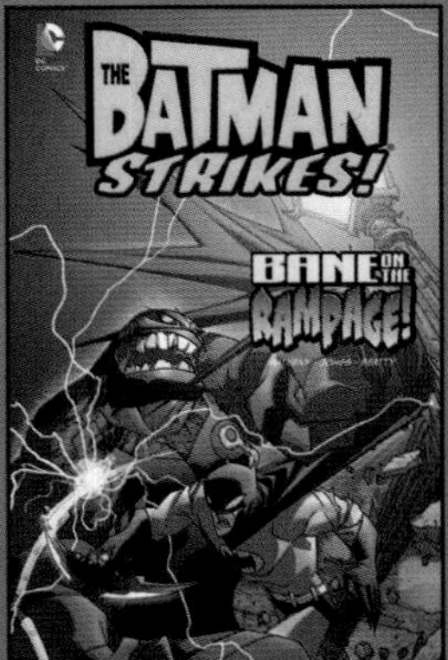
THE BATMAN STRIKES!
BANE ON THE RAMPAGE!

THE BATMAN STRIKES!®

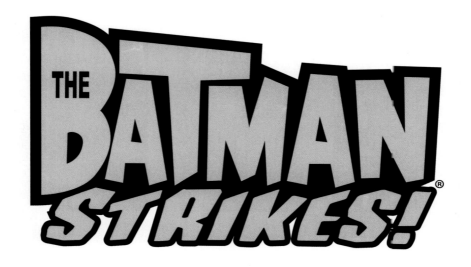